SANKOFA

A Culinary Story of Resilience and Belonging

by ERIC ADJEPONG
illustrated by LALA WATKINS

PENGUIN WORKSHOP

The last class bell rang, and Mrs. Boone watched as all the children packed their bags with smiles on their faces, ready to go home to their families. But she noticed there was one boy who wasn't smiling: Kofi.

"And don't forget," Mrs. Boone said to the children, "Monday is our annual potluck lunch! So bring a dish that best represents your family's culture."

Culture.

As soon as Mrs. Boone said that word, Kofi felt a knot twist in his stomach. He had been dreading the potluck lunch all week.

On their way home, Kofi and his classmates talked about their dishes for the potluck. One boy said he was bringing in spaghetti and meatballs, another mac 'n' cheese. Kofi envied how easy it was for all the other kids to come up with dishes that the class would surely love. When it was Kofi's turn to share his dish, he told them he and his parents were still deciding.

But Kofi knew that wasn't true. He hadn't even spoken to his parents about the potluck.

"Well, I'm sure whatever you bring in will be great," one of his classmates said, and waved goodbye. All the other kids lived closer to the school, but Kofi lived farther away, in a different neighborhood.

Even though Kofi loved his family and all the food they made at home, their food was so different from all the dishes the other kids were bringing in. It made him feel even more like an outcast, as if he didn't belong.

As far back as he could remember, Kofi had always felt different, even from his own family. He was born in America, but his mother (*maame*), his father (*paapa*), his grandfather (*nanabarima*), and even his sister (*onuabaa*) were born in Ghana, a country in the western region of Africa.

He only knew about Ghana from the stories his family told him. To Kofi, Ghana seemed like a very different place than the city he was used to. They all called Ghana home. But Kofi had never even been to Africa. Home was a place he had never been to.

"Kofi, my beautiful son!" Maame called out from the kitchen. "Bring me a palmful of fonio from the cupboard and then set the table for us. Paapa will be home any minute from work. He's been working all week and needs a nice hot meal to feed his soul."

The family began eating, their conversation filling the air in between big bites of delicious food.

"*Wo ho te sɛn?*" Paapa asked in Twi, his native Ghanaian language. "How was school today, Kofi?"

"Well, um," Kofi began, the knot in his stomach turning. "Mrs. Boone asked everyone to bring in a dish for our class potluck next week . . ."

Kofi watched as both Maame and Paapa put their forks down. *Silence.* He knew this was not good.

"And what day is this potluck, Kofi?" Maame said, breaking the silence.

"Monday," Kofi said.

"Monday!" Maame shouted out. "Kofi, *adɛn*?" she said in Twi. "I wish you had told us sooner. Your father is working all weekend, and I have to volunteer at the church. There's not enough time for us to just whip up a dish. And we'd have to make another trip to the market . . ."

Again, *silence.*

"I will help you, Kofi," Nanabarima said.

And just like that, the same knot in Kofi's stomach began to twist again.

"We'll go to the market first thing in the morning and let the ingredients speak to us," Nanabarima continued.

"Speak to us?" Kofi said.

"That's right, my dear Kofi," Nanabarima said. "Every ingredient has a story, but you have to know how to listen. I will teach you. Now finish your food before it turns cold. Your mother worked very hard to give us this meal, and we shouldn't waste it."

Kofi lay in bed that night looking at the moon—the same moon that hung over Africa, thousands of miles away—waiting for sleep to come his way. His mind was filled with lots of thoughts. He was anxious about going to the market, a place he had never been, with Nanabarima, a man he hardly knew despite being family.

SATURDAY

"Do you hear that, Kofi?" Nanabarima asked.

Kofi listened as vendors spoke quickly to each other and to customers. Some spoke in Twi. Some in English. Some in languages he had never heard before.

"Those are the sounds of our people," Nanabarima said as he watched Kofi look around the new world before him.

"When I was your age, Kofi, *me maame* would take me to a market just like this in Kumasi," Nanabarima said.

"Where is Kumasi?" Kofi asked.

"Kumasi is a city in Ghana," Nanabarima explained. "I was born there, into the Ashanti tribe, which means that you, too, Kofi, are a member of the Ashanti tribe."

"I am?" Kofi said.

"Of course you are! You are the son of *wo maame ne paapa*. And they are both Ashanti, just like me and my parents."

"But I've never been to Africa," Kofi said.

"You will . . . in time. But you don't need to go to Africa to experience it . . ."

Kofi eyed all the vibrant colors of spices. Nanabarima explained how each spice mix is a combination of many different plants and herbs.

"Are some better than others?" Kofi asked.

"They are all unique in their own way," Nanabarima said. "That's the beauty of spices. Each spice has its own story to tell."

"Breathe in deeply and tell me what you smell," Nanabarima said.

Kofi breathed in deeply just like Nanabarima had said to. At first, he didn't smell much, when suddenly . . .

"See, Kofi," Nanabarima began, "the harvesters take fresh turmeric, peel it, boil it, and then dry it out. Once it dries, they grind it into a powder and add other dried spices, like fennel, calabash nutmeg, grains of Selim, and cinnamon. We pride ourselves on being resourceful with our food, even when there wasn't enough to go round. To make the limited food as delicious as possible, we learned to use spices. Curry is a mix of different spices. Each spice is important on its own, but when blended together, they tell an even more wonderful story."

When the duo arrived at the next vendor, Kofi saw three different colors of plantains: green, yellow, and black. Nanabarima explained how the green ones are unripe and need to be cooked before eating.

"They are perfect for making chips and fufu!" Nanabarima said.

"And what about the black ones?" Kofi asked.

"Taste one," Nanabarima said. "Let the plantain tell you its story."

Kofi peeled a black plantain and took a bite, when suddenly . . .

"See, Kofi," Nanabarima said, "the harvesters pick the plantains from the tree at just the right time for ripeness."

Kofi and Nanabarima made their way to the rice vendor next. Nanabarima told Kofi about all the different types of rice: "Some grains are long. Some are short. Some are white. Some are brown. And just like the spices, each rice has its own purpose and its own story."

"What is this one?" Kofi asked
as he picked up a sack of rice.

"That, my dear Kofi, is Carolina Gold rice," Nanabarima said. "It's some of the best rice in the whole world. And it's grown in America. But it wasn't always here . . ."

"How'd it get here?" Kofi asked.

"I will tell you the story."

Kofi held the rice in his palm and let his mind drift . . .

"In the 1600s, our people were captured," Nanabarima began.

"They were led against their will onto ships, torn away from their families, and forced into slavery. To enslave someone is to claim ownership over somebody else's life, controlling what they can do every day.

"Before they were captured, some of the enslaved people braided rice into their hair, hoping to have something familiar to grow and eat when they arrived in the new land. That new land was America."

"But our ancestors were resilient. That means they had the strength to carry on even under brutal conditions. They were still able to find meaningful ways to connect with one another, to their African roots, to their culture . . . even though they were no longer home. And they often did this through food.

"They were given very little. They only had scraps of food that their enslavers didn't want. But even though they didn't have much, they knew how to make the most of the ingredients."

Kofi took a long moment to himself.
It was the first time he had heard this story.

"Our ancestors brought their spices to America," Nanabarima said. "They were the ones who grew plantains here. And they were the ones who cultivated the land to grow rice. Without our ancestors, these foods wouldn't be here today. This is why we must understand where we come from to understand who we are. The story of food is also the story of who we are. And you should be proud of who you are."

"I am proud," Kofi said.

"Then why didn't you tell Maame and Paapa about the potluck lunch?" Nanabarima asked. "Were you ashamed of your culture?"

"I guess . . . I . . . ," Kofi began. "I've always felt so different from the other kids at school, and I didn't want to feel any more different by bringing in food that they had never tasted before."

"My dear Kofi," Nanabarima said, "you will soon learn that through food there is more that connects us than separates us. I promise you that. Now, let's go home and cook. I have something I want to show you."

"This cookbook is our family's oldest heirloom," Nanabarima said, handing the book to Kofi. "An heirloom is something that gets passed down from one generation to the next. My mother gave this to me. And I gave it to your mother. And one day she will give it to you," he said.

Kofi held the book and read the title. *Sankofa.*

"In our language, Twi, we have a saying: '*Sankofa w'onkyir.*' It means that we must look back into the past for traditions and stories that have been left behind," Nanabarima said. "Otherwise, our culture will vanish."

Culture. There was that word again.

But this time, there was no knot in Kofi's stomach. In fact, there was a warm swelling in his chest. For the first time in a while, Kofi felt like he belonged. He was proud of who he was and his African culture. He couldn't wait to share his dish with his class.

"Now, let's get cooking," Nanabarima said. "We've got a meal to make!"

And so, the two began cooking, letting the ingredients speak to them.

MONDAY

"This is jollof. It's a dish from Ghana, my home in West Africa," Kofi said to the class. "And I have a story to tell all of you about all the different ingredients in the dish."

Mrs. Boone watched as Kofi told the story of his people, of the dish, and of his African culture to the class. A great big smile ran across Kofi's face.

Jollof Rice

INGREDIENTS

1 large Spanish onion, roughly chopped

2 Roma tomatoes, roughly chopped

1 teaspoon anise seed

½ large red bell pepper, roughly chopped

½–2 Scotch bonnet or habanero peppers
(optional, depending on how spicy
you want it)

2 garlic cloves

2 ounces fresh gingerroot, peeled

4 tablespoons neutral oil, such as vegetable
oil or canola oil

1 medium Spanish onion, medium chopped

2 heaping tablespoons tomato paste

½ tablespoon curry powder

1 teaspoon smoked paprika

1 teaspoon ground nutmeg

2 bay leaves

Salt to taste

2 cups rice, rinsed (Carolina
Gold or jasmine preferred)

1 tablespoon coconut oil

1½ cups stock (chicken, beef, or vegetable)

EQUIPMENT

Cutting board

Knife

Blender

Heavy-bottomed pot with lid

Wooden spoon

Whisk

Kitchen towel or aluminum foil

A NOTE FROM THE AUTHOR:

Before making this recipe, make sure to have an adult help and supervise along the way.

DIRECTIONS

In a blender, process the large onion, chopped tomatoes, anise seed, bell pepper, Scotch bonnet or habanero peppers (if using), garlic, and ginger until smooth.

Add the neutral oil to a heavy-bottomed pot over medium-high heat, and cook the medium-size onion, stirring often, until translucent, about 4 minutes. Add the tomato paste, curry powder, paprika, and nutmeg, and cook for 3 more minutes. Add in the tomato mixture and bay leaves, and cook down, whisking occasionally, for about 40 minutes or until most of the liquid has evaporated. (You're looking to cook the raw flavors out.) Season with salt.

Add the rice and coconut oil to the tomato mixture and stir the rice constantly to "toast" it for 5 to 7 minutes. Add the stock, and cover with a kitchen towel or aluminum foil and the lid. Simmer over medium-low heat for 15 to 20 minutes or until the rice is done, stirring at least twice during that time.